The Paper Princess Flies Again

with her dog!

ELISA KLEVEN

Tricycle Press
Berkeley • Toronto

Not so far away, in Mexico, a girl named Lucy loved a paper princess. Although no thicker than a leaf, the princess was full of stories.

"I'll always remember the day I flew with the butterflies into your town," the princess told Lucy one morning. "I'd traveled so far from the girl who first drew me, from the boy who gave me wings, from the cold snowy winter."

"And you looked so torn and tired when I found you," Lucy added.

"So you made me my dress like the sky," said the princess,
"and my strawberry shoes, and my flowery crown, and my dog."
She patted the paper dog who lay stretched out beside her.

"He's a good dog," Lucy said. "A little too plain, though.
I should paint him a colorful jacket."

"Why do I need a jacket?" the dog spoke up. "I have my warm brown coat."

Lucy thought. "You need a jacket because...tonight we're going to have a fiesta! Everyone will dress up, and we'll dance, and drink hot, spicy chocolate, and break a big piñata full of sweets. I'll make you a new jacket and give the princess a gift, too. Let me go find my paintbrush."

"Lucy is so good to us," said the dog. "We should give *her* a gift."

"Lucy loves stories," the princess said. "We could tell her a story."

"*You* could," said the dog. "You're clever and brave, and you've had so many adventures. But I don't have any stories."

"Let's see if we can find her something else then," said the princess.

Helped along by a passing breeze, the two friends skipped outdoors.

"How about this?" asked the dog, pointing to a bright paper flag on the ground.

"Great!" said the princess. "Lucy can pretend it's a little carpet."

"A flying carpet!" cried the dog, as a sudden wind
whisked them up.

The princess laughed as they sailed over towers and trees. But the poor dog trembled. "It's scary up here," he whimpered. "There's nothing at all to hold onto."

"Hold onto me," she reassured him. "And I'll hold onto this." The princess caught hold of a rippling ribbon…

tied to a soaring string...

fastened to a twitching kite belonging to a smiling boy. "How did my kite get these extra ribbons?" he wondered.

"We're not ribbons," the princess protested, straightening herself out. "We're a princess—"

"And a dog," said the dog.

"A princess? A dog?" said the boy. "Let's see." He tugged the dog from the kite string, tearing his hind leg.

"Careful!" snapped the dog.

"Sorry," said the boy. He ripped a piece from the paper flag and bandaged the dog's leg with it.

"Now you've torn Lucy's gift, too!" said the dog.

"Lucy's our girl," the princess explained. "And we should be getting home to her."

"But I want you to come home with me," said the boy, folding the paper flag around the princess like a shawl.

"I have an idea," the princess said. "Why don't you make your own princess and dog?"

The boy held the dog and the princess tight. "But what if mine aren't as friendly as you?" he asked.

"They'll probably be much friendlier!" growled the dog.

"Yikes!" said the boy, letting go. Away they ran on the wind.

"You were so brave," said the princess.

"Uh-oh, I don't feel so brave right now," replied the dog.

A coyote with hungry eyes had seen them flash by. "Tender little rabbits for my supper," he said, running so close they could hear his fleet feet and feel him panting down on them. There was nowhere to hide, just desert all around...

and nothing but one prickly tumbleweed rolling by.
"Quick!" said the princess. "Slip under that!"

Just in time! The coyote pounced, and the tumbleweed stuck him. "*Ouch!*" he howled, "You rabbits are bony and tough!" He stopped to lick his paws...

and the tumbleweed tumbled on, carrying the dog and the princess along with it.

"What a ride!" cried the princess.

"I'm getting dizzy," grumbled the dog. "And where is this tumbleweed taking us? What's that giant, jiggly place up ahead?"

"Oh no," said the princess. "I'm afraid that's the sea."

"The sea!" yelped the dog. "We haven't a chance! The water will swallow us up!"

But they found that the tumbleweed just bobbed on the water, jolly as a beach ball.

"We're still here!" said the princess.

"Here in the sea," gasped the dog, shaking salt water from his coat. "Now what?"

"I suppose we'll just drift," said the princess, trying not to sound as worried as she felt, "until something else happens."

"But I want to go home!" said the dog. "I want to give Lucy her gift, and dance at the fiesta, and wear my new jacket, and see the big piñata full of sweets."

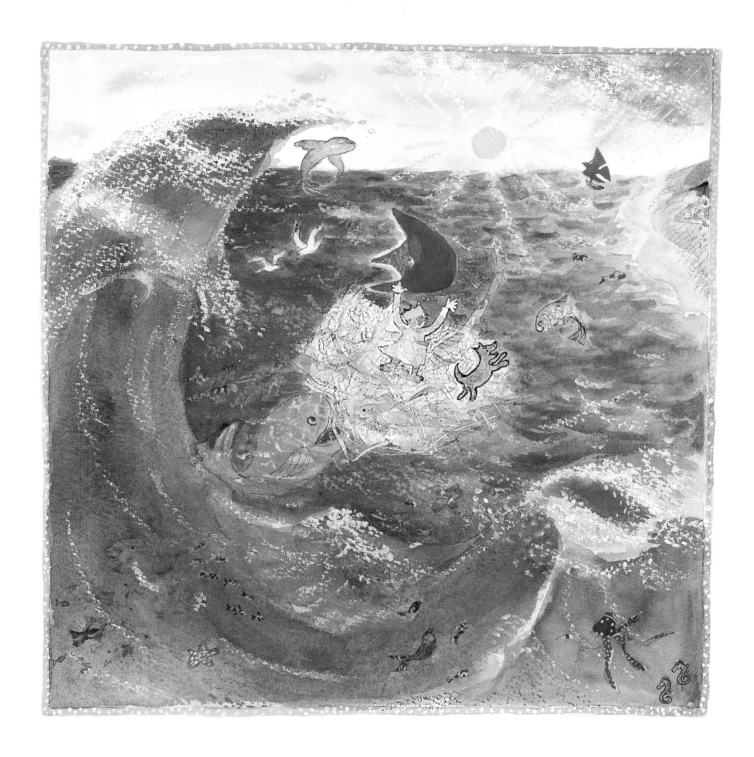

"Look," said the princess, gazing at the horizon, "a sailboat. Maybe I can flag it down."

She waved the paper flag wildly, but the sailboat slipped out of sight.

"Oh, I wish we had a sail," she said.

The dog's eyes brightened. "A sail!" he said. "I think we might have one."
The flag filled with wind...

and the tumbleweed skimmed toward the shore.

The friends cheered as their feet touched soft, warm sand.
"Now home!" said the princess.
The dog sniffed the air. "I smell cooking. Hot, spicy chocolate,
like Lucy's mother makes."

"But where *is* home?" the princess asked, as they drifted toward a town. "It's getting so dark and it's starting to rain."

"And the wind's picking up," said the dog. "We can't blow away again now."

"Quick, let's duck in here," said the princess, scrambling into a
basket full of brightly wrapped sweets.

"Do you think we'll be home for the fiesta?" asked the dog.

"There's always a chance," the princess said. Then, tired from
their travels, they curled up beneath the paper flag and fell asleep.

The princess and the dog slept soundly. They slept so soundly that they didn't feel the woman scoop them up, along with some sweets, and pour them into a bag. They didn't feel her carry them home...

or stuff them into a big piñata. They didn't hear her say, "Our
Lucy's been so sad all day. I hope the piñata will cheer her up."
They didn't wake up until...

SMACK, a stick hit the piñata. CRACK, the piñata burst open. Out they tumbled, with the sweets, into the light of the fiesta, into a ruckus of laughing and shouting, into Lucy's hands.

"My princess! My dog!" she cried. "You're back."

"We are!" said the princess. "Though I'm not sure how we got here."

"We brought you a gift," said the dog. He held out the paper flag, now smudgy and torn from its journey.

Lucy liked it anyway.

After the party, in the quiet of her room, Lucy gave her friends their gifts: a new dress and crown for the princess, a jacket for the dog.

"I wish we had something more for you," said the dog. "All that travel and we come home with a ragged scrap of paper."

"We do have something more," said the princess. "Something Lucy loves."

"A story!" said the dog. "*Our* story!"

Lucy's eyes shone. "Tell me!"

And deep into the starry night, they did.

With thanks to Nicole and Abigail

Tricycle Press
a little division of Ten Speed Press
P.O. Box 7123
Berkeley, California 94707
www.tenspeed.com

Design by Tasha Hall, based on an original design by Sara Reynolds
Typeset in Bernhard Modern, Lemonade, and Novelty Script

Library of Congress Cataloging-in-Publication Data
Kleven, Elisa.
The paper princess flies again : (with her dog!) / Elisa Kleven.
p. cm.
Summary: While looking for a birthday gift for their owner, the paper princess and her dog travel
on a kite, a tumbleweed, and a sailboat, and end up in a surprising place.
ISBN 1-58246-146-5
[1. Princesses—Fiction. 2. Dogs—Fiction. 3. Birthdays—Fiction. 4. Toys—Fiction.] I. Title.
PZ7.K6783875Pas 2005
[E]—dc22
2004030089

First Tricycle Press printing, 2005
Printed in China

1 2 3 4 5 6 — 09 08 07 06 05